Gascoigne Mackie

Poems

Dramatic and Democratic

Gascoigne Mackie

Poems
Dramatic and Democratic

ISBN/EAN: 9783337335274

Printed in Europe, USA, Canada, Australia, Japan

Cover: Foto ©Andreas Hilbeck / pixelio.de

More available books at **www.hansebooks.com**

POEMS

DRAMATIC AND DEMOCRATIC

BY

GASCOIGNE MACKIE

(Author of "The Ballad of Pity," and other Poems.)

London :

ELLIOT STOCK, 62, PATERNOSTER ROW, E.C.

Clacton = on = Sea :

LINE BROTHERS, PRINTERS AND PUBLISHERS.

———

1893.

All rights reserved.

E.V.

C B

CONTENTS

THE NEW SPIRIT

The catalogue of common things

Is no more common, no more dull;

Not solely in the bird that sings,

Not wholly in the Beautiful

So-called, lives wonder and the hope

Of the great future; nay, the dawn

Of Science brings a wider scope:

Poetic imag'ry is worn

To shreds and patches, fain would seek

A deeper impulse, and renew

Lost ways of Nature; so with meek

And steadfast eye let me review,

B

And trace here with a truthful hand

The landscape at my feet.

                                    Behold—

A morning toward the close of March.

Grey clouds in sullen masses roll'd,

With patches of azure, overarch

The earth; and gusts of warm wind stir

The pregnant trees, and swell the seeds

Unseen, of Spring; while lovelier

Glimpses of sun athwart the meads

Wake song, and lend the grass a hue

Of livelier green—a hundred roods

Of vale and meadow I can view

Here from this knoll, till distant woods

Sink in the circling gray, and mist

Obscure the hills behind ;—what wealth

Of lights and shadows melt and twist,

Quiver with mirth and sport in stealth,

Linger and lengthen, quicken amain,

Play hide-and-seek with breeze and trees,

Race over the meadows and rest again

Beneath bare elms !

                    Our hopes increase

With every hour : fresh marvels wake

The heart to happiness, and send

A challenge to the soul to take

Plain facts, and use them for her end.

A mile away, a railway bank

Confronts the eye : when all is still

At twilight, and I sit and thank

The sinking sun, and drink my fill

Of quiet thought with all that is,

Lost in deep-breathing reverie,

Half waiting till an angel kiss

My lips to song : lo ! suddenly

Between the vision of my gaze,

The silence of the evening star,

'Mid drift of smoke and sunset-haze

Sweeps the leviathan afar

With thund'rous echoes, ringing rods

Of steel, and force devouring space.

O, surely men shall be as gods

Knowing the Good and Evil, place

Their feet in pride upon the globe,

Ransack the mysteries of the earth,

While Nature's splendour like a robe

Clothes this more glorious second birth :

Old things must pass, the mind expands,

Parochial beauty, selfish joys

Dilate, the general heart demands

Expression. Shall no fusing voice

Chant in plain strains the strife and stress :

Man's work for man, life leased anew,

The progress through the patientness

Of the great dead, our fathers, who

Laboured in secret for us ? Yea—

A mighty nation at my back

Pushes me forward, bids me say

(Albeit these youthful tones must lack

The classic poise) that "man ascends

From step to step by slow degrees

That cannot lapse : ample amends

Wait upon effort ; this that frees

Binds by new laws, sure laws for ever,

The relentless laws of liberty.

Man's link with Nature none can sever,

Man's mastery a fool may see."

'Tis sung aloud by storm and cloud

And cleansing cataract;

The Race is born to Empire

That can grapple with the fact.

ENDYMION'S APPEAL

Clasp me for ever in thy silent arms,

And press thy sculptured lips close to mine own,

So shall I need no other love but thine:

For all the woods are wild with choirs of birds,

And every lake has leagues of whispering reeds,

And o'er the foam the mermaids faintly call;

E'en the vine-tendril tightens: O my love,

Mine unseen love, I am thy chosen one,

Faithful but mortal still, smit deep and sore,

For ever waiting and for ever sad:

Thou would'st not have me quit thee for a maid

Nurtured in men's abodes, e'en though her form

Proudly should move, with all love's argosy

Impearled, or lightly spread her laughing sails

To the passionate gusts of Spring — Lend me thy
    strength

To walk immortal on these heights alone;

With thee my soul can scorn the ills of life,

Without thee, I am as the sliding stream

That purls a wayward course mid flower and fern

Down through green dingles to the deep beyond:—

The lowliest find love's equal and a home,

The dead are with the dead, companions all

In bliss or sorrow: only I perforce

Am ravished with impossible love of thee,

Striving to reach up with my wingless arms:

O awful goddess, whose cloud-sandal'd feet

Have paced a thousand centuries away,

Watching this earth wheel fiercely on and on

Through death and change revolving; dost thou stoop

To stab with beauty an ephemeral youth,

Whose voice but deepened, when thy mysteries

Bade hush his saucy notes? — no skylark now,

Warbling shrill dawn-songs 'neath an April sun,

But stern and resolute: nerve and sinew set

To wrestle and to race.

                              O why, white witch,

Wilt thou not let me live as other men?

Why should I loiter on this lonesome steep,

Why bivouac under stars innumerable,

Innumerable stars and liquid chasms

Of silent peace? whence issuing from a cloud,

Thy naked grandeur breaks upon my watch

And whirls me heaven-ward, and I know not where,

Only this ecstasy will slay me soon;

And other shepherds, as they wind at dawn

Up the thin mountain-path, carelessly singing

Of kine and harvest-home, the pastoral life,

Will start to stumble on the form of one

Too heavily sleeping, to be called and hear.

Ah, but thou lov'st me, else I could not dare

To raise mere mortal eyes and gaze on thee;

Thou lov'dst me first; while still a careless lad,

One night in sleep the strange ambrosial musk

That marks thine advent, and all other gods,

Stole through my senses, and the world was changed.

I woke at dawn and longed to sleep again;

And when I slept, I cursed the chain of sleep

That showed but held me from thee.

But at last

Thou didst descend and fold me in thine arms;

I felt the life-beat of the universe,

Pressing mine ear against thy breast; I clung,

And let thy deity raise me from the earth,

Only by thee supported: ah! what bliss!

In thine austerity glowed deeper fires

Than loosed-lipped dalliance can excite by wine

Or languid cadence; thy firm mouth could tell

Of ecstasies beyond the scale of song,

Where silence sweeps the cosmic chords of love,

Spirit with spirit subtly interfused,

Speech without language, wisdom without years,

Untrammelled, fearless, though the shoreless heights

Together ranging, in majestic joy,

These were our nuptials.

                     Thou didst promise once,

When first thy sovran voice rang through the mists

That cap these hilltops, and I felt the thrill

That bade me upward glance:—Wilt thou forget

That promise, for to give becomes a god,

And mortals need the gifts immortals give?

Grant then, dear goddess, this request of mine,

Redeem thy words, leave men their treachery;

Make me thy seer, and hide within my soul

The comfort of thy secret: though no more

Mine eyes may watch the pearl of thine approach,

Do not deceive me, else may I become

Irresolute and irrational and morose,

Or seek to lose myself in lower love,

Who now am filled with infinite content:

Thine image must not wither like a dream

When one awakes, nor vanish with the shapes

That filled my cloudland-boyhood long ago,

But throb for ever in this heart—thy home.

Fair are the forms of women; none like thine

Have stirred my soul with glorious energies

By subtle contact, when deep waves of joy

Roll their triumphant crests along the sand,

And flood this sense-bound shore, my body; ah!

If not with thee, yet in untrammelled vision

Alone, still let me feel the gods gaze down,

And breathe with us from their serene abodes;

So am I constant still if thou art kind,

For ever humble and for ever glad.

KEATS

Severn ! where is the bottom of such grief ?

Say ! what can calm my heart's tempestuous heat ?

These throbbing temples knock for Death's release,

Aye, that word Death's my only comfort now.

Say me not nay, nor strive to win me back,

Dark Charon's mantle flutters at my side,

And soon must Iris slit the slender thread

That binds me to this body.—Tell me, friend—

But no ! Give me the laudanum, give it me

I say ; this farce is deadening work for you !

Day after day to play the woman thus,

To feed, to nurse, to watch, night after night :

The case is hopeless, Severn, let me die,

What is the world to me or I to the world !

A dream, a dream—the fifth Act's far too long.

Severn, you are the only friend I have,

And you I hate to keep. What am I worth

That I should waste the hours your Art should
claim ;

And yet you will not leave me, Severn ? no,—

Am I in Rome ?—the wonder of the world,

Necropolis of purpled conquerors,

Cradle of buried Cæsars.—Here are groves

Which Virgil and Mæcenas doubtless paced,

And shady porticoes which catch the North

Where Horace may have quaffed Falernian wine,

And praised his Sabine farm.—Am I in Rome ?

And I must lie here dying and see nothing !

O dust, rebellious dust, so silent now.

Where be those patrons and their fleeting clients,

Patrician, pleb, tribune and senator ?—

Vague names to fill a schoolboy's idle head.

Where be those gluttonous emperors, whose feasts

Amused my youth—and where those classic faces,

Warriors and statesmen, orators and poets,

Whose works and words the world has learnt
    by heart ?

Sooner or later we all come to this ;

What's fame and name and grandeur ?—Give us
    peace.

Play to me, Severn, that soft minuet

Of Haydn's soothed me much.—I seemed to see

A careful garden haunted by the dead.

Clipt yews and box-hedge, a long gravel-sweep

Of kissing chestnuts, and trim beds of flowers,

And a rosy arbour laced with eglantine,

And lilac fleeced with dew ; and lawns of grass—

Green English lawns, so common everywhere ;

But O, to one, whom sickness has stretched low,

How exquisite is e'en a blade of grass !

Alas, imagination will not stop :

I see a woman waiting for me there,

Her face out-pearls the moon, her locks of gold

Have leashed my straining soul, and these lorn orbs

Change colour gazing in those azure wells

Too deep for poet's praise; silence alone

And 'bated breath can give him strength to dive,

And sound the secret of his lady's eyes :

But I am weak—it was a cloud, a dream,

O God, let me not dream.

               But look there, see,

A fairy lights the other taper, see !

That's merry, Severn, merry, 'tis indeed :

Alas ! how small a thing can please the sick.

Once—once I vowed the moon should be my bride,

The morning star my bright-hair'd seneschal,

Like passionless Hesperus, my soul should brood

On beauty, free from love's consuming fang ;

Pan my apostle, and stream-haunted woods

Our happy home,—but oh, that dream has fled.

For long or e'er the face of man was seen,

Beauty knew sorrow for her paramour,

And Nature's nuptials are not lightly made,

Nor brook man's arbitration ; with them, Death,

Concealed behind the flaming torch he held,

As patient as a shadow, stood unseen ;

And as the pine torch wept, the shadow grew.

Has not some sculptor told the tale in stone ?

Ah ! Myths of Hellas ere mankind grew gray !

Ah ! Hierarchy of Gods Saturnian

That only haunt a poet's fancy now

Where are those manly forms of spring-tide strength

That tracked the fleet hart over dell and down,

Cheering their wild-eyed comrades to the chase

With bellowing horn; the wind-swept hills replying ?

Lost are the gracile shapes of boy and girl,

Wood-nymph and shepherd fingering happy flowers,

Sweet pagan figures of the Pastoral!

Save haply, etched upon some potter's urn

They pipe to us of white simplicity,

The violet cloudlessness of Attic skies,

A world of hyacinth and glossy bee;

In the morning of immortal loveliness

When summer filled the soul of Nature.—Gone,

Gone is that world's once naked innocence.

Why do we yearn for Hellas?—Yet 'tis good

To have felt the potent force of Nature bend

Our weakness to her glory, and our poor hearts

Fire with her solemn torch—none bade me write:

There are no masters of that Art divine;

Only the Spirit scoffs and buffets us,

And some supreme ideal in the brain

Tells to the trembling hand what words to trace,

But oh, when traced, how vague, how nugatory:

Yet still we persevere, still hope to catch

Some fragment from the feast of harmony.

c

Though long or o'er the song our souls desire
Float down, death comes, life like a bubble breaks,
And men soon cease to know that we have lived.
And yet we need no pity. Nature breathes
Her consolation on her children, and
Comforts the o'er fraught heart ; on her relying,
The pageant of the world swims like a dream ;
There never was true poet who fear'd death :
Rather we burst life's sensuous chrysalis
And greet the Angel's consummating touch
With mingled curiosity and awe.
Whether we sleep or live beyond, 'tis well,
What Nature hath ordained must needs be best.

The grandeur of a man is in his soul,
And how he faced the forces of the world,
And battled with himself—his tendency,
And not his finished work proclaim him great :
Did he maintain the majesty innate,

The inmost soundness, the inherent force

Of possible perfection in the race ?

Did he speak out the truth, and hint the path

Down which the coming generations, winged

With plumes of fiery hope, shall crowd and press ?

The glory of a poet is to stamp

An indelible mark of natural faith and love

Upon his epoch—this I have not done :

But I have lifted up the sacred hem

Of Nature's loveliness, and sung the truth

That dwells with beauty—more I might have done,

But full completion was denied me. So,

Whether men call me great, or scorn my work,

Rocked in the cradle of adversity,

I eased my soul of golden melodies,

And pointing to the gate called Beautiful,

Sleep,—Stretched at Nature's feet for evermore.

CHATTERTON'S DESPAIR

(Dedicated to J. A. S.)

This day of the week, tradition bids us know,

Died He who had no care to save Himself,

This day of the week will Thomas Chatterton die,

Having no care to live.

                     Had Barrett written

And sent me what I wished, had Beckford lived,

Or had the printers paid me what they owed,

Or had I owned one friend worthy the name,

I would not do this; hear me! in the future,

Printers and pimps should set up stock together,

For both are traffickers in human flesh

And prone to strangle immortality

By secret tricks of trade; listen and laugh!

Sixteen good songs for half-a-guinea cash;

Fell, Edmunds, Dodsley—all the crew of them,

Willing to tap my brains—Did Junius write?

I, Decimus, could match his stinging style,

And for that matter he's a purblind fool

Who cannot find a feasible argument

On either side, I found them sharp enough:

Since Churchill was in vogue, I had a fling

At satire too; the "County Magazine,"

"Middlesex Journal," "North Briton," "Freeholder,"

All knew me well enough :—Beside that work

Which claimed my deeper powers and grew in sleep.

O yes, I've struggled, but the dogs of Fate

Draw round their quarry, I am brought to bay:

Here in this dingy attic I must die:

Four months in London have I starved and sweated;

Hear me posterity! could a man do more

Than this boy did, or nurse a braver soul?

Only last month I spent my hard-earned pence

To send my mother and my sister something

Just as an earnest that I had that power,

Which given the chance, should lift us out of want

And they should live to praise the Bristol boy,

And share his fame.   O but my life has been

One brief ambitious stare : too proud to bend :

To crave a favour, stoop to menial toil,

Too proud :   For to the mystic lady-Muse

I vowed myself a dauntless chevalier

From earliest childhood.   Has it led to this ?

Dost thou betray me, while thou let'st those live

In affluence, who fleer and desecrate

Thy godlike image ?   Rise, thou haughty Sphinx,

Smite them, but let me soar.

                    And I might soar,

Could I but stomach Mother Angel's tripe

Given me for charity, because she knows,

" I'm looking pinched : She will not press for pay,

Because she sees I'm poor," she says "and starved."

She bade me once " Go to and be a clerk,

And earn my bread like any honest lad,"

Sit like a monkey on a three legged stool,

And live by tottles!   Pah! she turns me sick;

Her sweaty brow and fat square podgy fingers

Greasy with cooking, make me shudder: Ah!

'Tis strange this psychic hand should have to waste,

While hers grows red with plenty: she has that,

While I must sup on this which now I take.

—Not yet, let's reason.

                    Thoughtful Seneca,

Brutus and Cassius, Romans, perished thus;

Thus Cato, stern and calm: So Chatterton

Crushes his agony with stoicism—

For there's a limit which man's fortitude

Of suffering can endure; but past that point,

The affronted will disdaining to be shackled,

Dungeon'd too deep in dreadful misery,

Finds a sure freedom by another way,

And none but brave men dare to tread that way.

I will not weep, nor cry: "For pity's sake,

Give the young Poet bread,"—I want no pity,

For to need pity is a pitiful thing,

And mark of mean birth. No! I will lie down

Unconquered. Even the weakest woman knows

There are some snares more terrible than death,

A captain scorns to quit his sinking ship,

Dishonour slays a soldier more than death;

And I, shall I submit? Never! Needs then

I fare to-night where hunger cannot hunt me,

And where the sting of pride is never felt,

And vain the lust of self-idolatry;

Fame's herald cannot parley at those walls,

Nor shake the gates of everlasting sleep;

Come death! Thou seneschal of rebel dust,

That wait'st on all, in turn. Not yet, not yet,

Let me pull back the blind and seek a sign:

Alas! the skies are very pitiless,

God seems quiescent, and those stelléd fires

Are void of comfort for me; all is blank,

Nescient of sympathy and desolate.

Mercy! how have I made what fatal error,

How lost the thread in life's dark labyrinth

To stumble on this den?

                    Come, I will dream,

And memory shall mock at misery,

And beauty share with hunger all I have.

This mouldy attic vanishes: I feel

The sharp salt wind go whistling past my ears;

I'm on the gorge at Clifton; far below

The sluggish Avon crawls, on th' other side

A forest frowns the sun goes down behind:

Behold me in my yellow stockings stand,

And garb of Charity. O curséd Fate!

An antique soul lodged in a stripling's frame,

What care I now? is not thought free as death?

The wizard twilight holds me with a spell;

I seem to see great warriors in the air,

Mail-clad, on wingéd coursers snorting fire,

I their magician; when I give command,

They wheel and charge, or fall into the deep;

And far away to the West looms a vast band,

Deep-dyed in sunset robes, half-gods, half-men,

Harping of chivalry and battles old,

The castled pageantry of feudalism,

Cathedral pomp and monkish vespers swelling,

Rent standards flushed with many a bloody fight,

In glorious hurly-burly; while my soul

Glows o'er the grand confusion, and is calm.

What are the prizes of small life to me,

The pitiful tricks, the narrow shallow limits

Of the mean pence-clutching mediocrity

In the town below; when at the freak of will,

I'm lord of legions and the realms of thought?

Master of these, I scorn that lower world.

Must I bow down before the Juggernaut

Of Mammon ? No, who will may temporise,

And wear a Janus-face,—but I cannot.

Let me go further back : a different scene :

The nearer to the dawn the greater hope :

But twelve years old, yet hard at work at home

In my own attic, where with parchments old

From Canynge's Cofre, books and chemicals,

I the young Faustus toil'd ; O happy days,

With none to break upon my reverie,

While hour by hour on Redcliffe opposite

Towering I gazed ; till antique images

Of monk and warrior marshalled in my brain,

A secret birth I would not deign divulge.

Shall I forget that evening ? while I worked,

My sister knocked, I would not let her in ;

She said, " A letter for you ;" up I jumped,

Unlocked the door sufficient for my arm

Thrust through, to seize it ; and as I broke the seal,

I swore from sheer excitement. 'Twas from Walpole.

Here was the friend, the heaven-sent friend I craved,

The courtier-wit, the learned man of letters,

Whose kindly hand might help an aspiring youth;

Bristol should never hold me after this,

To London, to London, throbbed my heart.—I've
come,

I've seen, I starve—but Walpole lives!

O bed whereon I fall no more to rise,

Posterity shall judge who is the forger,

My lips are silent, justice is not here.

I'll not repent, defiant to the death,

For what I could I did and I have lived.

O double world, so hard to harmonise!

Eighteen brief summers is enough, I'm tired,

And very very hungry, but not mad,

Come to my bedside, mother, your boy is dying

Alone; O take my hand and close mine eyes,

O cruel world! you cannot hurt me now.

Bristol is far away, and home, dear mother !

Alas ! I was not all a son might be,

But you could never understand my ways,

And no one understood—they called it pride.

It may be I shall wake and live again,

And love, and Heaven forgive. But who can tell ?

Delusion, and delusion, and delusion,

It may be death is a delusion too !

Farewell ! You'll live, for you were never proud.

    Will he not come home again ?

      No, he is dead,

      Gone to his death-bed,

   All, under the willow-tree.

IN THE SHADOW OF THE CHURCH

Turn, my beloved, let me speak a word.

Katherine, the die is cast, and day is done;

No tears! in silence let our last farewell

Be taken, for it is most weak to mourn

For that which hath no remedy but death.

I'll not repent, what have we to repent?

While life is life, and love life's lonely prize,

Why should we weep that we have won that prize,

Though but to lose it? as a flower that withers

At sunrise. Go!—but do not go : still, still,

Would I enfold thee in mine arms, and rain

Salt tears till all creation swim in mist.

Would I might die with gazing on thee, Katherine.

God made me man but man hath made me monk,

God made thee mine, but man hath come between,

So runs this transient episode away,

Love's labour lost ; home, home, a ruined hope.

My dreams lie buried in the wilderness,

Joys scattered on the barren dunes of time,

Proud thought o'erthrown—and beauty doom'd to
   dust.

Thine hazel eyes will haunt me in my sleep,

Thy form swim twixt the chalice and the cross,

Thy brown hair touch my cheek, when bowing low

In fast and supplication, I implore

Mercy for sins that I have never known.

Go to thy homestead duties, I to prayer

And lonely cell and austere vows must turn,

To pore on ancient missal, and the Word,

And mutter misereres for the dead.

Did not the holy Master claim too much,

The impossible ? O what most haggard deeds

Hath not religion been persuasive of ?

I would I were a painter for thy sake

To limn thy face above the chancel, there

To smile for ever with the holy Babe

Upon thine arm, of motherhood divine,

Worshipped by thousands with adoring palms;

Alas, no art is mine, only the pang,

And endless pity for thy withered youth,

For thou wilt never wed, though I am gone :

Sundered and silent, time will soon flow by.

Thine eyes are shells still trembling with the spray

Of seas celestial, flung by envious waves

Upon these temporal coasts; soon, when the tide

Rolls up, they will be gathered back again,

And sink once more into the deep unknown;

Whence issuing once, they told a wanderer

Of other lands and seas beyond the sun.

Life hath two scales, one Mammon's and one God's;

And when this is depressed, then that is raised;

The heavy cross flung in the fleshly scale

Will lift thy soul to strike the stars on high,

So art thou nearest heaven in deepest woe,

Gethsemane's the porch of paradise;

Katherine, farewell, the trial of faith is ours.

Katherine, farewell, still silent.—God is Love.

D

LINES ON AN OLD MAN READING

He sits in his arm-chair;
Sunk are his eyes, and somewhat dulled perchance;
The features scored and trenched with many a furrow,
Scars in life's battle, now to end so soon:
Scanty his locks and white: his clothes hang loose:
Creased his hand-veins and swollen; all the marks
Of powers fast-failing recognisable:
And yet he reads, with one foot in the grave:
And round that snow-capped hive the busy bees
Of thought still hum; and with the month's fresh
    flowers
Crowd the o'er-brimming brain-cells, e'er the frost
Of winter warn that working-time is done.
Why such activity then? for we may guess
That none on earth shall share this aftermath,

In the world's busy mart his place is filled:

" Peace for the old," they say, " with meditation ;

For us new generations, yours is past."

And yet he reads ; and will none benefit ?

Mere waste, mere plethora of Nature's store?

But in the old man's face there shines a light:

"I still am younger than you think, my friends :

And trust the instinct, for God does not jest.

It may be, when my twilight closes in,

And bees no longer hum around this hive,

But dormant lie in seeming death, and feed

On the sweet labour of the summer months ;

That I, like them, shall find good use for all,

Nothing superfluous, mere pass-time nothing.

It may be I shall need my knowledge then,

And in new worlds act out experience here ;

For all God's works rise on a gradual scale,

From good to better, and from better best:

Doubtless our use of life here must determine

Our station in the next—if next there be.

The economy of Nature will not waste,

Cannot afford to waste, one man's good hive ;

Here being needed, for a while I stayed,

That there, being needed, I may win a place,

And work my way through progress infinite.

I'm not so old as you suppose, dear friends ;

Though I must leave you, and with some regret,

And one world at a time is the wise plan ;

Still I conceive no reasonable doubt

But that these cells shall pour earth's honey forth,

And in the fadeless fields of asphodel

Barter therewith for other honey, good

Alike for them, as their's will be for me ;

From nothing, nothing comes. Wherefore, my friends,

Ply with your busiest wing from flower to flower :

Store up, store up, fill your capacious hives,

And garner knowledge while the sun is yours ;

Aye till the curfew toll 'tis not too late:

Perchance, the last blithe truant laden down

With nectar, while the rest are snugly housed,

May bring the costliest essence of them all,

Whom to have lost had been great detriment."

ON THE MULTIPLICITY OF POETS

"A locust-plague of poets now," one cries :—
"As grains of Lybian sand innumerable."
"Countless as the billows of Atlantic seas
That arch their scornful crests where no shore breaks
The grandeur of their limitless succession."

The critic groans "He cannot drain the sea:"
But better thus : "Profound Immensity !
Loved boom of sullen thunder in mine ear !
That trumpet of defiance to the winds
Which only deep and massive waters blow,
Is born of drops of salt confederate :
O who could wish a breaker less ? e'en bells
Of foam that scud before the rousing breeze,
Vacantly irridescent, hint the stress

And strife of pushing waters underneath,

While e'en the third-wave breaks incontinent:

But where's the loss? Old Neptune still roars on.

Just so the complex choir of Britain now,

Say rather of the world's democracy,

Is grander in its multiplicity

Than any single voice of simpler days:

Sweet was the oaten pipe Sicilian,

Matchless the plastic plainness of the Greek,

Meek Maro's tender majesty; the swoop

Of him whose phœnix-dust Ravenna guards,

How swift, how final! Never has the voice

Of singing ceased since that eventful dawn

Which smiled upon the jocund company

Of pilgrims bound for Canterbury :—But

Cephissus, Tiber, Arno, Thamesis,

Now blend their rich-ored individual streams

With the sad thunders of a coastless sea:

One everlasting oratorio

Born of slow-heaving waters submarine,

Of multitudinous waves, and buoyant billows,

Of scum, of broken surf, and tossing crest,

Mounts up, breathed from the common heart of all ;

And Neptune laughs to hear his children sing.

So let the sea-cow bark.

RURAL LIFE IN ENGLAND

By John Self, Rhapsodist.

1

I'll tell you how our village looks
In England at the summer prime,
My knowledge is not gleaned from books,
Or abstract thoughts of the sublime :
No ! but by communing and prayer,
From hour to· hour, from day to day,
During the magic month of May,
With Nature in the open air.

2

E'en now the bursting blaze of gold
Blinds my weak eyes with dizziness ;
I see the champaign fold on fold
Panting with bliss and loveliness ;

England! dear garden of the North,

Whose sons are feudal, silent, proud,

Lords of the earth by all allowed,

She rears them here and flings them forth.

3

At dawn,—the window open wide—

The thrush, the cuckoo, and the lark,

By many a singer deified,

Are heard in every field and park,

No touch of grief is in their tone;

But should you hear the nightingale ₁

Plead low to the stars, and pause, and wail,

You'd feel how men still suffer wrong.

4

In May the chestnut's stalwart bough

Builds up its pyramid of light,

The first to leaf, the first to strow

Its sailing petals left and right,

The bower of many a missel-thrush :

Then, too, the lilac white and grey,

Bursts, blossoms, weeps, and fades away,

Scenting the air at sunset-flush.

*   *   *   *   *

5

I see the red-roof'd cottages,

The smoke curls up—how blue and straight—

To-morrow will be fine, it says,

Or should be fine ; at any rate

'Tis better not to dogmatise :

The swallows skim the cattle-pool

Where cows are standing sleek and cool,

Flicking their tails to scare the flies.

6

There is a fragrant smell of milk,

Mingled with wafts of wild dog-rose,

Sweeter to me than all the silk

In which my scented lady goes :

Where is the city's boasted charm ?

Take all the treasures of the realm,

Give me a hawthorn and an elm

And health upon an English farm.

7

The villagers, when work is done,

And when the thickening twilight lends

A beauty to the setting sun,

Loiter around the corner ends,

Smoking and gossiping at ease,

Their brains are never overwrought

Or harassed with religious thought,

They live and die in frugal peace.

8

The sombre yew-trees close at hand,

That guard the barrows of the dead,

Preach lessons all can understand,

Though beauty robs them of their dread :

The common course—the common fate—

The churchyard grass is wet with showers,

And bees are busy in the flowers

That mark the term of man's estate.

9

Death stamps a prescient majesty

Even upon the brow of want,

Death binds by ties of sympathy

The learned and the ignorant :

The proud Patrician lined with gold,

The Peasant-labourer in his blouse,

Meet, massed in death's impartial house,

And recognise a common mould.

10

The pride of race is being spent,

Democracy is taking shape,

And he who boasts of long descent

Is only nearer to the ape.

Let brother take his brother's hand,

And own we are of equal stock,

Nature can build a rampart-rock,

By welding grains of simple sand.

11

What makes the splendour of the field?

'Tis not a solitary flower,

The waste of time to which men yield

Lies not in any single hour:

A drop of rain is not a shower:

A man,—be he however proud—

Is still but one among a crowd,

It is the mass that makes the power.

*   *   *   *   *

12

Many a half-hour one may pass,

Stretched in the meadow at full ease,

Amid a countless sea of grass,

Slow, undulating in the breeze:

Imagination unconfined

Here proudly mounts where will may lead,

Can make a cloud an Arab steed,

And gallop with the rushing wind.

13

A touch of Nature's magic wand

Moves thoughts of manlier majesty

Than all the learning of the land:

Simplicity's enough for me:

To catch the wild lark's morning call,

Or take a solitary jaunt

To hear, beneath some leafy haunt,

The streamlet's flowing madrigal.

14.

Long, long, too long I've felt the weight

Upon me of the cultured age,

Now with a shout, I spring elate.

And claim my lawful heritage:

Let poets file their dainty words,

And filigree their Watteau-phrases ;

I sit and wanton with the birds,

And sing among the summer daisies.

15

Nature, divinest Mother, so

May strength with undisturbed repose

Attend me whereso'er I go,

And calmness bring at evening-close :—

And grant, ere thy enshadowing wing

Close o'er the twilight of my days,

That I once more may sing thy praise

With worthier imagining.

SEEDS OF PROGRESS

By John Self, Rhapsodist.

The wind was warm to-day, and smelt of spring,

The sea as faint with some long reverie,

(Her white limbs still half flushed with ecstasy

From the sun's lordly revels) slept secure,

Only one handmaid-seagull hovered near

To tend the sleeping queen—yet not alone

The ocean, but the land itself looked fair:

I know that buds will break on every bough,

And hope lend lustre to the tender blade,

E'en now along the thicket I descry

The noiseless midges weaving their airy loom;

Joy throbs their tiny hearts; the rooks are loud,

And lesser starlings fly innumerable

Across the labour of the plough, to peck

Food from the new-turned glebe; all birds are glad,

E

A tantivy of gray pigeon from yon holt

Clap the warm light, pursuing and pursued.

O mother, mother, why this mystery?

Have I not served thee well?—and yet so mute!

Love's tears will dim thine April violet,

The flossy bud of primrose hear the brook

And wake with spring, aye, every stick and straw

Will feel th' exultant thrill, and welcome give.

Shall I alone forget thee, and be mute,

Pass by in silence?   Ah! I know not why,

The dawn of beauty is akin to pain,

And love doth wake in fear, no sensuous shaft

So poignant as the arrowy glance of spring.

Why do such mornings stir sad memory,

O why the bird's sweet note, unbidden tears?

What would'st thou have me cry, dear mother, speak!

My heart is pure to listen, quick to catch

Thy subtle whispers—may I say a word?

I did not come from nothing as ye know,

I am a part of what I see around,

For all I see seems to my inner sight

Arrested man—and thus my love expands

Till aspiration kindles into act,

And act reacts in wider sympathy

With all that is.   The timeless distances

That loom behind the least make him appear

Both small and great: small in the sum of things,

And great as having that to use at will,

Which millions of long years have gone to make.

I am not as an evening nightingale

That sings of sorrow all alone, and flings

Her solitary song away in haste,

And drops in silence with the shrivell'd leaf ;

If I am strong, my strength is also yours,

If I am joyful, you will share that joy,

The past has sown the flower that springs to-day,

A plain meek man who cannot be dismissed.

The great world-spirit seems to chant again,

The pulse of poetry to stir anew

To grander issues; if it once seemed good

To lock a fairy in a lonely line,

To carve a crystal cameo; now no more:

Dazed are mine eyes, my throat too thick for speech,

Good bye to fancy, give me fact instead,

The bald and terrible scientific fact,

This fills me with a hope that transcends all,

A hope, an insight, aye, a certainty!

Ha! for the rose's blood beats in my blood,

The beasts my cousins, and the birds my kin,

With every tiny elemental wing

I claim connection; for the world streams on,

Creation does not falter, all that is

Strains forward and improves from day to day,

A grand and infinite complexity

Based on broad unity of cosmic law,

No split, no sundering, but resistless force

Working in solemn order, upward ever;

Why pant? why hurry? what is there to fear?

Man's imperfections lessen day by day,

The chariot of the world's democracy

Wheels slowly on; the pigmy Phaethon

Who held the reins of Empire for a day,

Drops headlong; but Apollo never falls.

Think you that God in Piccadilly dwells,

Or yawns from clubland on wet afternoons,

A varnished cynic shod in patent shoes,

Grown weary somewhat of the ways of men?

No, no, the kingdom of the poor draws nigh,

The Philistine is on thee dandy Dick,

Look to thy brains and not thy pedigree;

For the workman stares his master in the face,

And those who sat in darkness see a light,

And there is something in the souls of men

That cannot be down-trampled, nor bought up,

Nor patronised, nor pauperised, nor scorned,

And woe to those who will not recognise

That something; for it does not dwell in one,

But in the race : Nature is prodigal,

And will attain her end at any cost.

The sky's no longer like a crystal case,

With a circling sun to warm the good flat earth,

And man as master ; nor the stars no more

Mere points of flame to light the bell-man home ;

Things were not made merely for man's desire,

To serve his ends : his minion or his thrall.

" Break me my heavens," quoth God, "and let
    me see

Their boasted glory shrivel in the gaze

Of world on world, innumerable, proud,

Swifter than sight, whereof their pigmy earth

Swims like a bubble (albeit of my breath)

Upon the waters of the universe.

Ha, these upstanding men that seem so great,

Of magnet atoms marvellously moulded,

They shall grow greater by another fall.

Witless you laughed, you killed my herds and flocks,

You raised yourselves an inch above the rest,

And made your God, a man ; my world, a board

To serve your appetites ; enough of this.

Know now you cannot kill a jot of mine,

My power fails not, no atom ever dies,

It cannot die, for I am in that atom ;

My progress marches on with steady foot

To certain triumph ; the music of my laws

Your ephemeral thunder mocks, you wake to sleep :

And pass like shadows wailing bitterly,

Cramped in your cast-iron creeds, until some flame

Heat the same atoms to another shape :

Then shouting you proclaim, "Behold the truth,"

But truth is meek and comes not with a shout."

The spirit of democracy is mild,

Wise without learning, full of sympathy,

Has no desire to quarrel about creeds,

Wishes none ill as long as they will work;

All work's the same with her, no small nor great

Her heart expands and is not envious,

Her soul as ancient as the naked stars,

As unashamed as Nature.   'Tis her joy

Not to decry the storied majesty

Of saint and hero, king and conqueror,

The pomp and pageantry of feudalism,

The cloistered lady, the romantic love;

But she refuses to regard the world

As satan-bound, and sinful at the core:

Rather she feels God breathe through everything,

Making and moulding all to His good end;

And all men help him who do honest work.

For 'tis the man that consecrates the deed,

And not the deed that magnifies the man.

Democracy has no desire to slay,

Does not pull down, but rather levels up,

And wants no prizes in another world :

"O in this life" she cries "life to the full,

And quench the thirst of curiosity ;

The costliest foe of man is ignorance."

Wherefore, chant forth, my soul, in faith and love ;

And mix thy rivulet with the rushing river,

In the great whirl of things take thou thy place :

For now the night of sorrow dies away,

And creed and caste are melted in one flood

That rolls its mighty billows, crest and foam,

And tonnage of tremendous waters, on,

Till God's democracy emerge at last

Self-governed, self-controlled, speaking one speech,

Slaves of the lamp of love, and therefore free.

FERDINAND

A quiet wash of water; moon, and miles of sand;

Horror of solitude; God, Death, and Ferdinand.

"Hear me, Thou Lord of life! For am I not thy
    child?

Hear me, by whatsoever name best reconciled:

Prime Force, Creative Cause, Jehovah, Great
    Unknown,

I cry, waste-bound I cry, alone with Thee alone.

The waves' hoarse diapasons mock me. Who am I?

Sperm-germ of cuckoo-spittle—Man —O let me die.

For oh, to what vain end would art strain out
    life's tether?

Tis but a little folding of the hands together.

What of the night? Speak, watchman-star!"—
    "The night will pass,

And morning break:"—"and wax and wane: all flesh is grass!

In vain I tread the crowded square, I pace the wild,

To find one human face, calm, perfect, undefiled.

I see but incarnated shards and shreds of lust,

Legions of lost souls, hungry miracles of dust.

Oh for ablution." As he spake, he moved to meet

Ocean: white tongues of surf broke hissing round his feet.

"'Tis O for a new creation, a dream that we have not dreamt,

A life of manifold action, if any were worth the attempt.

Novelty, novelty, aye, till everything novel must seem

But infinite variations thrummed on a threadbare theme.

For the tale of the earth is told, and girdled the earth's strait scope:

The fabled chest is exhausted, and science has strangled hope.

Automatons all as it seems, in body, in will, and in mind:

Destiny handles the tiller: necessity sits in the wind.

We compete and defeat one another: we labour and know too much:

Our passions are frittered in folly till deadened is Nature's touch.

The Apple of Love is eaten green; we are flaccid ere ripe,

We huddle and bubble together, till we trend to a pigmy type.

We force and we forge our children to gather untimely fruit:

To know if the brain be growing, we pluck it up by the root.

And most are as grasping as feeble; methinks that there is not one

Who dare read by the inward lamp, or will suffer and stand alone.

I hate this base generation of baby-egos and boys,

This mart of mouthing and mammon, of belial-
babble and noise :

This age of smatter and smartness, of cunning
shallow and 'cute,

Where the silt of civilization scarce covers the
naked brute.

But thou, dread death, art firm : turning to thee,
we cease."

Slow swell'd th' voluptuous wave, and coil'd and
pluck'd his knees.

"O to see a new sun rising out beyond some unknown bay,

O to hear the wild birds singing far away, and far
away :

Watch the planets flush at twilight over some
marmoreal sea,

Muse upon the cosmic vision where no fool can
follow me.

O my soul is lost in sorrow, sick with sighing
for mine own,

And my cry to God and man is simply to be left
alone.

Will they never cease to bicker, bite and blacken,
    fret and fume ?

O to hear the trump of God blare out their
    everlasting doom !

I should laugh to see their fulsome vices
    hypocritical,

Like the masks from actors' faces when the play is
    over, fall :

Scan them naked and astounded, know them as
    they really are,

See their pseudo-philanthropics weighed before the
    judgment bar :

I should smile to see the man who sneers and
    cavils at the throne,

Battens on the sins of others, strive to justify
    his own :

See the journalistic braggart curl up like a
    frightened louse,

See the editorial ' we ' shrink back as modest as
    a mouse :

See the pariah and the pauper, see the outcast
    in her shame,

Stand above the worldly-wise man, step before the
stately dame :

Would the heavens might sink in thunder, stars
splash, earth and ocean gape,

That the gods might close for ever th' annals of
the human ape.

Alas, vain is this loud lament—vain these sighs."

And now the rising sea plunged heavily round his
thighs.

"O that I had not been born into this æon of
arid woe,

O that I had lived and flourished half a thousand
years ago.

In an age when life was joyous, somewhere in
the sunny south,

When a passionate love of beauty passed in song
from mouth to mouth.

Would that I could quit the stricken city, and
in lieu of woes,

Lie enchanted in the golden garden of Boccaccio's ;

Laughing at his tales of frolic with their sly
insouciance,

Loll at listless ease, and eat the lotus-leaf of
indolence :

Vernal maidens such as Botticelli painted would
be there,

Sprightly as a host of lilies, breeze-blown lilies
debonair.

Lo ! I seem to see before me in a vision at my feet,

All the youth and yeast of Florence masquerading
in the street.

See them pass ! their reeling flambeaux stream
against a sallow sky :

Dainty comfits, darts of cupid fall in showers
incessantly :

Posies toss'd from tinsell'd casements pelt the
surging crowd below :

Damsels borne on milk-white palfreys, nodding
gaily as they go :

Frescobaldi, Soderini, Salviati—all are there—

Private feuds are drowned in revel, naught is
banished now but care.

'Hail Lorenzo! Lord of freedom: Hail Lorenzo!
 he is ours,

Welcome May, the month of madness! Florence
 hails the month of flowers.'

'Hail Lorenzo!' Lute and cymbal clash and echo
 from afar:

Gallants dight in silken doublets follow his
 triumphal car.

O'er the bridge while Arno trembles to the cresset's
 fitful flare;

See! the dome of Brunelleschi shadows half the
 central square.

'We defy thee, death, thou dotard! while our merry
 pageant goes:

Haste, haste, carnival is passing. Pluck the lily,
 strip the rose.

Haste! the spool of time is turning: Maidens,
 make no long delay,

From the tangled floss of Fortune spin the
 brightest thread ye may.'

Voice by voice, the minstrels catch and lift the
 measure as they go,

F

While the lyric-shuttle weaves the web of music
to and fro.

O'er S. Marco, shriller fragments, as the choric
voices swell,

Smite Savonarola brooding lonely in his cloistered
cell."

"But such pageants ceased.   And Florence was
not merry any more :

All her wild hozannas silenced by the cannon's
shattering roar.

So, youth's democratic fancies, passionate visions
of redress,

Pass like pictures.   Hemm'd and harass'd stands
he silent in the press.

Poor and disenchanted : now he seeks for
sympathy in one,

Marries in a blind delusion : wakes to find himself
alone.

Vainly he maligns his fortune; pressing wants
and cares obtrude,

And the fight for sheer existence scarcely leaves
him space to brood.

All his soul's lustrous enamel, all th' ideal's pink
veneer,

Rubbed and worn away by living in the city, year
by year.

Thwarted by a thousand worries, petty pothers,
paltry strife,

Selfishness at last becomes the ruling motive of
his life.

Cased and crusted in convention; pillar of a
palsied church :

All his nobler speculations left for ever in the
lurch :—

Aye, we know the type of pillar, plethoric with
dews of grace,

Unctuous pillars, whitewashed pillars, bald and
broadest at the base !—

Now he ridicules his earlier vision of a perfect state,

Prides himself on being purely practical—and never
late !

Late ! ah me, the ways of mortals seem so sad,
so comical !

I can scarcely weep for laughing, laugh for
weeping at it all.

Pitiful pathos, fierce philippic; which is timelier,
    who can say?

While we watch the rising waters wash the sands
    of time away.

Oh, my soul, thou ancient river, thou hast
    trodden down man's strength:

Aye, that ancient river Kishon rolls us all away at
    length.

Harrying, hurrying, marrying, burying, where's the
    wonder, where's the worth?

Comes at last the staid procession, sable steeds,
    and dropping earth.

Ah! these spaces stretched above me seem
    surcharged with speechless fate,

Ah! this 'scintillating, silver, shimmering sea
    disconsolate!

Man might be a king of beauty, man might fill
    a god-like throne,

Could he learn himself to choose the law of nature
    for his own.

But we imitate a copy, dare not be ourselves at all;

Or we deviate from nature, just to seem original.

O ye sapphire chasms of splendour, tell me
whither, tell me whence;

Shout the answer, echo, echo—I defy the
consequence."

But from the void vast night rang out no answering
note,

Albeit the bubbling tide had risen, and lapp'd his
throat.

"Out of the east and the west swell the sounds
of disconsolate wailing,

Wailing of infinite woe: sounds of interminate
sighs.

For the heart of half of the human race is a prey
to delusion:

Ignorance, mother of sin, rules in the street and
the square.

Round and around like a mill-wheel the nations
from sunrise to sunset

Toil; and a turmoil of tears is life; and death is
a sleep.

I know, if stayed, I too like a straw should go
down in the maelstrom:

Therefore with soul undefiled turn I, dear mother,
to thee.

Out of the ivory gate have the sanguine illusions
of boyhood

Fled: but a dawn of despair breaks in this desolate
town.

Thousands of cynical swords, and legions of
devils beleaguer,

Banners and brass of the strong storm round this
sorrowful fort.

Alas! there are traitorous curs too that lurk in
the citadel smiling,

Whispering, " Better to yield, better surrender
than starve!"

Nay, by the deeds of the dead. I swear that I will
not surrender,

Therefore, inviolate death, turn I for refuge to thee.

"I will open the wicket of sleep, I will pass to the
garden of Lethe,

Under the trees I will stretch, hearing the
nightingale sing.

Where the winds and the waves sweep never, nor
sign nor season revolving

Comes: but immutable calm rules, a perpetual
queen.

Under the boughs of the broad crepuscular cedar
of silence,

Couched upon sorrel and rue, lost in monotonous
gloom:

Alone, I will ponder at dreamful ease where the
shadows lie longest;

Marked from the boisterous crowd—waiting and
watching alone.

Nor folly, nor fever, nor fret, nor favour of
fortune shall find me

There, where the hemlock flowers whiten and wither
intact.

Flush in the fruit, and bloom from the bud, and
the falling of blossom

Pass, but no change is felt. Summer and winter
are one.

Quiet security rests like a spell o'er the spot, and consummate

Silence sombre, and deep shade, and incurious sleep.

"Courage! ere I pass for ever let me chant a palinode.

Some by right are heirs of Belial, some are saints and sons of God.

Some are born to sink in sin, and some are framed to shield and save;

Æons of ancestral influence make and mould us from the grave.

Aye, and living, mere suggestion can induce a waking trance,

And another guide our motive, lord of life and circumstance.

But the puppet, self-deluded, poses as a freeman still,

Speaks of sudden intuitions, while he serves a stronger will.

What is overmastering genius but an automatic strain

Of the racial instinct somehow summed up in a
single brain ?

Many a link of dead endeavour joins the genius
to the dunce,

And he reaps in rich abundance seed another
scattered once.

Every kindred aspiration, every effort of the mind,

Goes to swell the consummation of the mission of
mankind.

Not a sin, a vice is useless; no experience but
must tend

By accumulated wisdom somehow to the wished-for
end.

As the Israelites of old went journeying onward
with the ark ;

Genius plants the human standard furlongs further
through the dark.

He alone, or some few with him, sees by night
the pillar of fire ;

And his eyes reflect that glory : dead : his ashes
still inspire.

" In the hour of deep disaster, when the cry is
· 'Ichabod';

Flash of faith. A single strong man. Nations thunder where he trod.

From the Jews' fell persecutions sprang the world's white aloe-flower:

Prophets, monarchs, priests, and martyrs prayed and passioned for that hour.

When He came: He was rejected, scorned His summons from above,

Hunted like a lonely partridge was the Lord of light and love.

True to-day the mediocre do not murder any more,

True, the Sadducean critics serve statistics, not the law!

So they cry: ' He's mad or mattoid, genius is akin to crime:'

Baby-savans, blasé cynics stab and sneer him out of time.

By the great ones gone before us, better freedom though in death;

Than to fester in the city breathing in another's breath.

I will tell the shades in Sheol: 'Merry England
    is no more,

Only smoke and squalid millions, miles of brick
    and mud galore!'

Faith has vanished from our faces: in this life
    alone, it seems,

Must the wise man lay up treasure: and forsake
    fanatic dreams.

Give us truth, whate'er the ransom for truth's
    freedom we must pay:

Yet I think our mothers were not wrong to teach
    us how to pray.

There a mystery unexplained still, and I hear it
    on the beach,

Ceaseless in these surf-tongues hissing at the
    seaweed out of reach.

From the deeper seas, an echo: 'Seeds are
    scattered everywhere,

And a soul of sterner fibre shall be born of thy
    despair.'

Ah! indeed, the individual withers, as the poet
    sings;

We must die content to grasp the righteous tendency of things :

Though so loath to hear the phantom knocking on the other side ;

We must pass, and let the others blunder where we used to guide.

Some-day, doubtless, somehow, though we shall not live to see that day,

Man's immortal aspirations will be summoned into play.

When our so-called education will not leave him, like a child,

Naked of bread-winning knowledge, hungry in a pathless wild.

When the curse of competition branded on the young man's brow

Will not find him old at thirty, as it often finds him now.

When the statesman will not turn the public trust to private ends,

Nor the homeless needy lady have to live upon her friends.

When the woman and the man shall stand as
comrades side by side:

When to help, not hoard the million, will be held
in highest pride.

When a conscientious thinker will not have to
quit his church,

Nor the callow curate clamour, like a parrot, from
his perch.

When distracted sects shall widen and unite in
love and zeal,

Christ identified at last with our humanity's ideal !

All these things will happen some day, in the
future far ahead,

Some day in the golden future, after you and I are
dead.

O to live and love again when æons shall have
washed us clean,

When this stormy world has wheeled into a cycle
more serene !

As for this, my Roman exit, let him judge who
understands.

God! if God there be: I give my body and soul
  into Thy hands."

A splash. A string of bubbles. A widening ring.
  No more.

Only a quiet wash of water on the shore.

A DEMOCRATIC CHANT

By John Self, Rhapsodist.

Behold! I will sing one great song from the depths
of my soul;

Of life: what it was, what it is, what it may be,—
the whole:

Not muffled with vague lamentation, not stammered
in rage:

Not beating void wings like a bird at the bars of
her cage:

Nor gazing with eyes from dim watching made sore
and distressed,

Not with burden of years of long labour and learning
oppressed;

But buoyant, as after a lapse of unsorrowful rest

On the lap of our wonderful mother, whose beautiful
breast

Lulls all her tired offspring to slumber with gentle
caress,

Who loves not her mighty ones more, nor her little
   ones less,

So impartial is she from whose temporal prison I
   break,

As free as from rock spouts a torrent, white-flashing,
   awake,

In joy of wild liberty leaping in headlong career,

Too strong to be stemmed, too liquid to pause, too
   swift to be clear,

But with frolic of foam-bell and froth and impetuous
   voice,

He cries to the highlands and lowlands: I flow,
   I rejoice ;

For the spell of the morning is on me, the mist of
   the heights :

From the womb of the mountain I spring, from
   impervious nights

In the dim underworld of deep darkness ; where,
   pent and at bay,

Meand'ring in mazy abysses, I forced my slow way

Through slate, slag, and shale : till behold ! I leap
   forth into day.

I ask not for smoothness, for idlesse: broad
boulders may block,

Pen, parcel and split: I accept them; with many
a rude shock

And buffet of cliff, I race forward somehow to mine
end,

Nor loiter to question and quibble whereto 'tis
I tend;

For the weight of my waters impels me resistlessly
on

'Neath the sunlight of labour, the magic of twilight,
of moonlight alone;

I swirl the green banks of broad meadows and
champaigns of corn,

Through forests of firs and through dingles and
dells where the birds sing at dawn,

Through great lone recesses, and chasms of un-
speakable gloom,

'Twixt drizzling black rock-reefs I gather with
thunder, and boom,

When all the blind bulk of my passion is hurled
forth apace,

G

(A polished white column of waters arched over
    sheer space),

Ere fountains of foam are dashed back again,
    shattered in spray :

But I shake my stunned senses, recover, and urge
    on my way :

Soon streamlet and burn, tarn and beck, bend
    their footsteps to me,

My brothers, my comrades, they join me, they
    long for the sea :

Though our sources be many, and voices may
    differ—in purpose and love

With one soul to one sea democratic united we
    move :

And who shall resist us persisting, who bind us,
    who block ?

They who cannot and dare not encounter are
    welcome to mock :

They may stand on the bank, wring their hands
    in despair, watch and weep,

And wail for the past that has flashed by for ever,
    may wail for the steep,

Whence our waters first rose, the pure well-head,
the fountain, the source :

And others may fear for the future, the close of
the course ;

For already the waters are salt with the tears of
the ages, and dull

With the turbulent billows of passion, blind
pushing, and clamour : and full

Of the poison and reek of the mills, and the filth
of the towns :

Oh ! what can the future avail, though they court
us and crown us with crowns,

If the waters we drink are mephitic, the flood
that we float on debased,

With all the morn's innocent dimple and shimmer
and dancing effaced !

Well ! so let them wail as they will, if their
faith be declined :

Yet still, O the grandeur of dust, the incredible
marvel of mind :

Outracing the gale, and defying the changes and
chances of time,

Deep-based on the laws now unriddled, the facts
    that are fixed, the sublime

Long labour, success of our fathers, who silent,
    yet speak !

O the endless progression of thought, from the
    schools of the Greek,

And the city of scholars deep-brained, who could
    gather the gift

Of the wonder and wealth of the past, who had
    patience to sift

And to hand on the best to the new generation,
    aflash with the flame

Of the glorified Nazarene's fire, whose immaculate
    Name

Shook down the strong thrones of the Cæsars, and
    set up in place,

Self-sacrifice sweeter than life, meek might of
    invisible grace.

Then came the slow struggles of creed, the age
    of the Councils, debates,

Fierce factions, malign persecutions, betrayals,
    intolerant hates ;

Still, under the crystalised dogma, the bull of infallible Pope,

Dilemma, and logic of schoolmen; the seed of humanity's hope

Grew in cloister and castle, cathedral and convent; the effort was one :

Monk, merchant, crusader and monarch, proud lady and nun,

They laboured, they fought, and they loved and they yearned for the best,

For the something Divine yet unconquered, the dream that would not let them rest,

Unsatisfied still, they grasped at the future, till out of the East

Rang an echo; "This earth is not wholly a snare of the Beast;

The beauty that lures thee in Nature and woman, the simple delight

Of innocent children, of homestead, and garden, is good and is right;

There is joy in the finite, the lisp of the least leaf may thrill thee, the hell

Of the Eremite's madness, the scourge, the
seclusion, the ban and the cell

Are marks of vain torture, of helpless endeavour
to break through the bond

Of flesh that imprisons, that bars thee from vision
of wonders beyond :

But the wonder is round thee, the dust that thou
spurnest is pregnant with truth,

The books thou contemnest of Hellas are blossoms
of Nature and youth ;

No longer gaze mournfully over humanity blasted
by sin,

No longer strive vainly to solve the sphinx-riddle
by searching within,

There is earth at thy feet, there is life in the
street, there are joys that are clean :

Go, mix with thy fellows, despise not God's
creatures ; th' unseen and the seen

Must mingle, enlighten, correct one another—thy
visions of love

Beyond, are not all—all that is thou must love
that the world may improve."

Thus grew the great Age of New Learning. There were feuds, there were fights

For freedom of conscience, for government civil, political rights :

And the wave of progression swept forward.

Then woke with a burst

From her feudal oppression a Spirit of marvel in men, and a thirst

For adventure and travel and knowledge of others, impassioned delight

As of children who gaze the first time on a glorious sight ;

They swept round the world, they ransacked the ages, translated and taught ;

They lived hard, they worked hard, they died hard ; they sought and they fought

For something they deemed very precious, not above nor beneath,

But for liberty dearer than life, and for love that is deeper than death,

Here, here, on this earth. And like Titans they groaned with ambitious desire

To wield from the heights of Olympus the bolt of
  invincible fire.

Then budded the rod of our Empire; aye, chips
  of the oak

Were the sires of the sons of the West, who have
  flung off the yoke ;

But one blood and one race with one speech are
  we still, and a time

Draweth nigh for a closer alliance to blot out the
  crime

Of that futile oppression.

                And then broke in battle a terrible dawn :

'Twixt the rights of a Monarch, the wrongs of a
  People, the kingdom was torn ;

Heaven guided that issue through triumph and
  failure : the struggle was stern :

But the strength of the nation was solid and patient,
  could suffer and learn,

Though a frost chilled the early success, and
  fanatical gloom

Wrapt all the gray island: but silently under the
    doom

Of depression and stillness, as under the cloak of
    the snow

Bursts a delicate snowdrop, that tells of the promise
    of spring,

Waxed the weak flower of science, a modest and
    tentative thing,

(While the rest of the landscape lay formless and
    featureless, pale as a ghost):

That clung to the earth, and was slow in its
    growth, hardly noticed by most,

But still there it was.

            And when Winter at last had gone by,

There ran a faint tremulous shudder through Europe,
    a sigh

Of oppression and hatred against the oppressor,
    but not a soul stirr'd:

And a voice of revolt against tyranuous priestcraft
    which nobody heard:

In revel by moonlight with courtier and mistress
    the monarch sat throned:

And under the feet of the monarch the angel of
  Liberty groaned:

"What are kings? what are rights? what,
  religion?" the sceptic enquired:

"Mere tricks of the stronger to harass the weaker,
  gross selfishness tired

And trapp'd in deceitful apparel—society's built

On a lie—back to nature and freedom." they
  cried: "let the guilt

Be avenged of their sons and their fathers: come,
  let us restore

The reign of the people primæval."

                              Then rose with a roar,

As of beasts of the forest when twilight is falling,
  a nation enraged,

And wreak'd their red fury in wreckage and blood
  till their wrath was assuaged;

Till out of their ranks climbed a despot, remorselessly strong,

A man of the people, who led them to glory, and
  Europe ere long

Lay flat at his feet. But he fell at the last, and
his deeds were as dust

That reddens a terrible sunset: the fame of his
reign and his lust

As the flare of a portent that flashes and fades
from the sky:

But the dream of democracy widened.

          And science arose,

And strode through the dark in the shape of a
giant, a giant that throws

The shadow of dread upon all that he passes: the
woods quake with fear:

At the sound of his footstep, the ring of his
hammer, the hills disappear;

He measures and mutters, the seas cannot check
his imperious stride:

He blows his great horn through the storm: as
he plunges his steel in the tide,

Waves leap to obey him, no darkness benights him,
he watches in sleep:

The roll of the ocean he changes to light as he
  lolls on the deep,

While all the huge weight of his mail the mad
  waters must keep,

Though they curl their white lips, hiss and heave
  in his wake, they must toil at command,—

Soon became the great gests of this giant a power
  in the land;

For his eyes were so clear he could tell what the
  stars were composed of, and note

All those little black minims that lurk in man's body
  to hurt him, and float

Else unseen, in the air; and his ear was so keen
  that no sound could escape,

But words that were murmured at Cairo he caught
  at the Cape;

But strangest of all were the tales that he told;
  for like Zadig the sage,

The hound and the horse that he never had seen,
  he described: and the age

Of the earth, and the various races of men, what
  they saw, what they prized,

Ere Memphis was raised from the dust, or the
tombs of the Pharoahs devised:

And he spake with authority too of men's faith
and men's fears;

"Aye, what were their creeds and their shibboleths
now in the ocean of years!

He had made all religion a science, could trace
how belief had evolved

Through totem and fetich and ancestor-worship:—
the question was solved:

And man's mind was a delicate web of gray matter,
priest-figment the soul;

His will but the ultimate strongest sensation that
governs the whole:

His freedom a farce, his crime a disease, and his
faith a fine folly."

So spake the dread giant, and straightway on all
fell profound melancholy.

Behold, I will sing of myself, for myself am a part
of the whole,

John Self, the waif of the hopes of his age with
the chant in his soul:

For a nation brought me to birth, 'tis futile for
them to disown;

For I have not sprung like a palm in the desert,
self-sown and alone,

But the desolate Past with long sighing and labour,
and passionate fire,

As he yearn'd for his shadowy Psyche, the Future,
his unseen desire,

Begat me: behold me, believe me, I am what
I am,

With the frame of my father who sleeps with his
fathers, but eyes lit with flame

Of the lady my mother, the deathless, the dauntless,
half-veiled and half-seen,

And I feel that she will not deceive or disgrace
me, my mother, my queen.

For oft, when the folds of the twilight have fallen
and covered the land,

In the fields I have wandered and pondered and
felt for her hand,

For the stately white hand of the lady my mother,
when roses are blowing;

And raptured with glory of summer and gloaming
moved on without knowing,

Till stealthily out of the scent and the mist and
the gloom of the wood,

In place of her hand, there has fallen a kiss on
my lips, and a mood

Of clairvoyance, ineffable insight, and buoyant
delight ;

And I know that the soul shall strive onward till
reason and love shall unite :

Till passion and purity blend, and the "ought"
and the "is" be as one,

Till love shall no longer be wild, nor knowledge
wax sterile alone,

Till the heart shall not shrink from the head, nor
the head be betrayed by the heart;

When the lion and lamb shall lie down together,
religion with art,

And the weanèd child shall place his hand on the
cocatrice-den,

Aye, faith shall not swerve from science, nor
science be faithless then.

The ways of the world without shall not war with
the world within,

Nor the fruit of the tree of knowledge be plucked
from the boughs of sin,

The apple of love shall not waste in the mouth to
the dust of remorse,

Nor the face of a thousand ships bear the freight
of a nation's curse.

Our girls and our boys will be brought up together,
no longer divorced,

United in wiser reliance on nature, not fettered,
not forced ;

The mind of the girl must be braced by the boy's ;
no more shall inanity

Strangle the growth of her best, or swallow her
talents in vanity ;

The boy will be touched by the grace of the
maiden, and sweetened in soul,

Till from knowledge of either arise something
better than knowledge—control.

The poet's heart shall not ache for the ways and
the days of the dead,

For the present shall thrill and exalt him when knowledge and love have wed,

No more shall his bosom heave like a salt and a homeless sea

Plunging in desolate search of the shores of eternity,

Nor shatter in cynical spray 'gainst the floes of the world's cold face,

Nor batten and waste on the drift of the wash of the commonplace :

No, no, O receive me, believe me, take back, 'tis thine own,

This faith in my soul, of the future prophetic : leap, leap to thy throne,

Reign there ! thou art king in the realm of thy splendour, no more thou art dust,

'Tis faith that must crown thee triumphant in effort : the ultimate trust

That dies unrewarded, that marks the divergence of manhood from beast :

And this in its essence may be the possession of greatest and least.

H

I sing not of heroes, for all flesh is goodly, alike
　　in the main ;

I claim no advantage of birth or possession, I
　　share what I gain ;

I stand with my fellows, I need them : together
　　we thrive or we fall,

The sin and the sorrow of one is the sorrow and
　　sin of us all :

Society holds us and folds us in fetters far firmer
　　than brass,

'Tis as drops of the ocean, as leaves of the oak
　　tree, as green blades of grass ;

'Tis the pageant of millions that moves us to
　　marvel, the measureless sweep

Of the fields of the harvest, the gloom of the
　　forest, the roar of the deep,

And my spirit in rapture flings forth a proud pæan,
　　caresses the whole ;

We lend to each other our best and our bravest
　　—I give you my soul—

Nay, 'tis not my soul, 'tis the soul of a nation
　　that beats in this song ;

For myself. I am nothing, I rank with the file, I
am one with the throng.

O Father almighty, Thou wilt not deceive us, Thou
wilt not protract

The night of our sorrow, the dream of our doubting,
the faith which we lacked,

For now through the mouth of this people and all
men by me thou art praised.

O mother immortal, dear earth, thy dark atoms of
matter are raised,

Mysterious, are raised in the scale of our knowledge :
we bow, and we trust.

O mother protean, immortal, abiding, that weavest
the dust

To shapes of full splendour through seasons of
wonder, maturity, rest ;

That buildest and breakest, that turnest and shakest
the mould in thy palm,

As of old thou wilt feed us and shepherd thy
chosen and shield them from harm.

Round these brows at my birth 'twas a bough of
green olive, of olive, not yew,

Thou didst twine as a sign of peace of the soul
thou would'st grant, not to few,

But to all who would walk in the ways of thy
wisdom and help thine increase:

And this promise to those who will follow and
serve thee—thy palm and thy peace.

SONG OF THE WANDERER'S RETURN

1

Hell, pack your fading fires,

Stars, freeze your worst:

I'll quench my deep desires,

I'll see my lady first.

I come, I come.

2

From rugged Russian floes,

Icefields and bears,

When scarlet dawn arose

Love heard my prayers.

I come, I come.

3

By Ganges' floating lamp,

Crocodiles cry :

Jungle and veldt and swamp,

World-wanderer I :

I come, I come.

4

Cast me your horoscope,

Stars overhead;

Lighter than antelope,

Hark, 'tis her tread,

She comes, she comes.

5

Thou art a woman,

I am a man :

Love, love is human,

Life is a span.

I come, I come.

6.

Tease me no more, ye Fates,

Under this dome!

Breathless before your gates.

I come, I come,

Love, take me home!

LOVE'S CONQUEST

1

Here let the billowy tempest overtake us
Of love, of love;
Here let his arrowy lightnings rend and shake us,
Time will approve;
Heaven comes not closer than a woman's heart,
Or none, or all, I crave! O love me not in part.

2

I am no false half-hearted wayward lover,
The passion comes:
I plunge, my foot not deigning to recover,
I love but once;
God-like should be the wooing lover's strength!
O let me anchor on this happy isle at length.

3

Nay! tell me not to move mine eyes away,

>> Dread not their fire :

Lust, sloth, and envy now have had their day,

>> Gazing, expire :

It is thy cleansing soul I hunger for,

It is the God in thee I yield to and adore.

4

Lift up these gates immortal, let me wonder,

>> Oh! have I won?

Mine, wholly mine, till life's stout bark go under,

>> The voyage done :

Lightnings may cease,—let joy descend in tears,

And this sweet rain make rich the hope of future years.

A FALLING STAR

Did sleep refuse your gentle eyes

Last night, and did you sit awhile

While moonlight filled the summer skies ;

And watching with a wistful smile

Still muse about that shooting star

You saw, while we were walking home ;

When fearful of hard days to come,

You gazed, and wondered what we are !

And fragrant memories at my heart,

Like violets drenched in April dew

Revived :—while hope, the nobler part

Of life, began to thrill anew ;

Sweet voices hailed me from the grave,

Far o'er the sea, where shadows shroud

Death's garden, and sheer cliffs of cloud

Blot out the dead whose names we save.

3

We children in life's pilgrimage,

What can we know? a pious guess;

But Eden-tones and sacred page

Hint something deeper than success :

Let us be clear : " We do not know,"

So falls that star ; and then perchance

From honest night of ignorance

A dawn of deeper truth may flow.

4

Life's not for victory or prize,

But effort only, as it seems ;

The will, the work, the enterprise,

And sunny days for sowing dreams ;

We sow, we reap; lovers and friends;

And what remains of cherished hours?

Only a knot of faded flowers,

And memory—so, so it ends.

5.

One royal moment on his throne

Love sits triumphant over death,

Calls the wide universe his own,

And lives an æon in a breath:

He mingles, mid that short delight,

With music borne from worlds afar:

Then, like an inharmonious star,

Swerves: and shoots headlong down the night.

6

We are but wanderers. Let us stand,

Though rains wash bare life's ruined pride,

And ocean swallow sea and land,

Though not a soul stand by our side,

Unbribed, unsuccoured, undismayed,

Still let us stand and conquer ;—aye,

The red rose withers on its stem,

What is life's final diadem ?

Death—love's last utterance—a sigh.

A HARMLESS DITTY

At dusk we took our walk abroad,

          O fie !   O fie !

I stole a kiss along the road :

          Tra la la, tra la le.

She blushed and would not look at me,

          O fie !   O fie !

And so I made the kisses three :

          Tra la la, tra la le.

And no one came along the lane,

          O fie !   O fie !

She gave me one o' them back again :

          Tra la la, tra la le.

Like me may every lover thrive,

          O fie !   O fie !

,I feel quite glad to be alive :

          Tra la la, tra la le.

ALONE!

1

Firm of purpose, God-reliant,

Parted and alone I sit:

Still the spirit is defiant,

Bleed on heart—what of it?

2

Doubtless love's a heaven-sent blessing,

Life's one peerless aloe-bud,

Still not given us for possessing,

What comes next?—Solitude.

LULLABY

1

O to fling down this weary head
'Mong valleys where they never reap :
A pillow of poppies for my bed,
And dream-dews from the Latmian steep ;

   Thy brown wings hover,

   Cover, O cover,

And shield me with thy pinion, sleep !

2

Sing smoother measures than the airs
That blow round Lesbos, famous isle,
Drop down, and take me unawares,
To roam and roam thy realm awhile ;

   Till night be over,

   And dawn uncover

My dreaming eyelids with a smile.

LOVE'S PATIENCE

1

Can the life be worth the living

That locks up the human heart?

Can the love be worth the giving

That surrenders but in part?

Life should be a generous giver

Full of bounty and increase :

Love, a slow, majestic river

Deepening through a land of peace

2

Can a man be worth the waiting,

If he dare not cope with fate?

Can a maid be worth the mating,

If too fickle-frail to wait?

So, my heart, I bend and kiss you,

Like a lover true and brave,

Though faith only see the issue,

Love will last beyond the grave.

LOVER AND MORALIST

,

LOVER :   Let sorrow come, I'll not regret.

MORALIST : Though love should wither with the
           leaf ?

LOVER :   It was in summer that we met.

MORALIST : Love's summer days are hot and brief.

LOVER :   The heart-shaped cherry on the bough

           Allured the glossy starling's beak :

MORALIST : Fit emblem how a lover's vow

           Can win and waste a blushing cheek.

2

LOVER :   Red breathless clouds streamed up the
           East,

           And hail'd the sun-god from afar :

           The thrill Earth felt within her breast,

           A thrush sang to the dying star ;

           Hark ! hark ! the lark's auroral cry

           That light as wine leapt in our veins :

           " All other raptures cannot buy

           The least of love's immortal pains."

THE COST OF VICTORY

1

Profounder peace my soul invades

    Than, after battle's blood and strain,

Lulls the broad field, when evening shades

    The silent faces of the slain.

2

There, hopes like stricken heroes lie

    Foe-facing, with their eyes aghast ;

Joys bivouaced 'neath the open sky :

    O joys! too proud, too young to last !

3

Alone, I pass across the field

    By moonlight, 'neath the tranquil trees :

God never meant the right to yield,

    'Twas worth the loss to gain this peace.

4

The splash of blood, charge and recnarge,
  The whirl and scream of shell and shot,
A man must meet: would he enlarge
  The kingdom native to his lot.

A ghostly combat 'twas, meseems
  By far the fiercest fight of all:
These sighing hopes and splintered dreams
  Shall claim most solemn burial.

6

With calm I count the fearful cost,
  And inwardly exult; although
I ne'er shall head a braver host,
  Nor gaze upon a fairer show.

LONELY LOVE

1

And if I love thee, what is that to thee !
Will not the sunflower bow toward the sun ?
What's one pale star when morning has begun,
And who in youth remembers memory ?

2

We met as friends, as friends we part again :
Go and be happy, break another heart!
Thou soon wilt learn to play that higher part,
And pride will teach me how to smother pain.

3

Ah me, I toil, I ache to comprehend :
O moon and sea, O stars and miles of sand
Where once we used to wander, hand in hand,
Nor ever wonder how it all would end ?

4

O wild-wood walks !   O fire of youth's ambition !

Alone with thee along the moon-lit corn.

That moon has fled, how bleak the fields stand
    shorn !

And cold neglect the meed of woman's mission.

5

Nay, but the heart is such a tender plant,

So sensitive to sunshine and to rain :

A gust will make that blossom shut again,

Nor future music as of old enchant.

6

Why teach me love if but to leave me thus,

That melody's too sad to sing alone :

Love aches to sit upon a single throne,

Her unshared honours how monotonous !

7

To wait while beauty withers silently,

Me, me, thy spring-tide's sweetheart left alone :

O home which once 1 thought to call mine own,

O phantom faces I shall never see !

AN AUTUMN SONG

1

What is this pang that strikes across my heart ?

A silent flush

On field and bush

No wild wood-thrush doth waken.

2

What are these tears that tremble down my cheek ?

Must I alone

Live on to mourn

My loved ones flown, or taken ?

3

What is this splendour streams across my soul ?

Fight the good fight,

We shall unite

When earth lies quite forsaken.

THE SAND-FLOWER

Where ocean breaks on either hand

Along a bleak and sterile shore,

Where tongues of surf lick up the sand,

Amid the wreckage and the roar,

Where heaps of blackened seaweed lie

Mid matted drift of various tides,

Which, as the refluent wave subsides,

Bevel the blue bald pebbles, I

Found this sweet blossom blowing.

2

There was no other verdure near,

Only the straggling thistle crawled,

And some few bents of salt bleached grass

Told to the wanderer who might pass

Of earth's last edge : where one might hear

The stormy seagull as he called,

And watch the full tide flowing.

3

The central strength of all we see

Has not this flower's immaculacy,

Yon seagull poised on outstretched wings

Still wants the scent this blossom flings ;

The huffling sea-wind sweeps and blows ;

This never argues,—but it grows,

And praises God in growing.

4

Sweet flower ! how keen was my surprise,

And not untouched by earnest shame,

To note you there with eager eyes,

And yet to never know your name !

By what mute gift, what subtle spell,

Could you transform with chymic power

Mere sandy waste and salt sea-swell,

Into this lovely lilac flower

I press within my bosom ?

5

And yet I need not marvel : for

In crowded cities far from view,

Pure souls fast locked by love's stern law,

Whose names not e'en the wisest knew,

Have lived ; and by some wondrous grace,

Some art of sweeter alchemy,

Some charm of rarest charity,

Have touched to life the commonplace,

And bade the desert blossom.

THE METAPHYSICIAN

1

The lonely scholar shut his book,
  And rose and stirr'd his dying fire,
Still standing, he began to look
  And watch the winter-day expire :
And as he saw the vapours roll
  Across the meadows far away,
Mesmeric twilight brimmed his soul,
  And filmed his eyes with ecstasy.

2

Through his mist-clouded window-pane,
  The tracery of twigs and boughs,
The leafless hedges rank with rain,
  Even the sheep-flocks and the cows

Seemed strangely still.—"Ah me," he cried,

"Is the world really what it seems,

Or are we cheated and belied

By incommunicable dreams?

3

"For now I feel so wierdly dull,

So plunged in doubts I cannot prove,

Lethargic and insensible

To this tough world in which we move,

That almost I am prone to say,

Gazing o'er yon grey waste of mist,

That th' ego is refined away

Sometimes, and ceases to exist.

4

"Why else this drear-eyed dreamy gaze

Over the fields at twilight tide,

If this life be not but a phase

Of some far larger life; allied,

Yet torn from which, th' atomic frame

   Obeys the spirit's plangent stress,

And deadens, while the yearning flame

   Flies forth into the wilderness.

5

" For all the fossil-forms that print

   Past strata of the growth of man,

Whatever mind or memory hint,

   I piece together as I can,

If haply—ah! but who can know,

   What single brain can grasp the whole ?

Where is the science that can show

   The structure of the human soul ? "

THE HEIGHTS OF WINDER

Red chanticleer's loud clarion calls,
   And chides the mists, and bids them pass:
Alike on loose unmorticed walls,
   On slanting roof, and sparkling grass,
Frost, like a million grains of spelt,
Glints, as the rolling vapours melt.

O valley of a thousand rills
   That falling, feed the dark main river;
O ring of proud and royal hills
   That stand consolidate for ever
'Twas ye, 'twas ye who rear'd my youth,
Who gave me strength and taught me truth.

3

These sun-smit summits, unperplexed

　By clouds blown crossways o'er the skies,

Fill me, by many a fancy vexed,

　With silent hope and deep surmise ;

Clouds too may loiter round the base,

But splendour fills the mountain's face.

4

Yon mountain doth not mock its star,

　Nor envy swell the lesser hills,

Content they stand for what they are,

　And laugh through all their lyric rills :

These steep'd my mind, or great or less,

　In something sweeter than success.

5

Something that cannot be o'erthrown,

　Methinks, this mountain doth express ;

A conscious might that stands alone,

K

A majesty, a gentleness,

Which bids me follow what is best,

Unchecked:—and leave to God the rest.

6

There is a Voice speaks in the air

Of worlds that lie as yet unproved:

A Presence o'er me everywhere,

Which will not argue but is loved:

A Message, howsoever sent,

Which is its own best argument.

THE TWILIGHT STAR

1

Lone lamp of twilight, vestal star so distant,

    Sole sentinal ere thy myriad sisters glow,

Star of the east, eve after eve persistent,

    Marking the spot whence dawn will surely flow :

2

Storms blow, and blot thee out from man's divining,

    Thou'rt lost, thou'rt gone, the sore faint-hearted say ;

And yet full well I know thou still art shining,

    It is the clouds, the clouds, which pass away.

3

O twilight star, symbol of light more tender,

    Star of the soul, guide of distempered youth ;

In sovereign faith I yield complete surrender,

    And henceforth follow in the track of truth.

4

Thou, round thine orbit, journeyest, never swerving

From that fixed course in which the planets move:

O soul, swerve not from that great law of serving

By which thy being mounts through endless love.

OFT IN ELYSIAN RAPTURE

1

Oft in Elysian rapture have I wandered

O'er dell and down, through glen and grove,

Where'er my footsteps led me, I have pondered

The royal song, the perfect love.

2

Alas! what lips of clay can ever sing us

The song of songs, the royal chant?

And who of mortals breatheth that can bring us

The love of loves, the love we want?

GOOD-NIGHT—NOT GOOD-BYE

There is a word that wrings the heart,

    And oh! too soon it must be spoken,

It comes when those who meet must part,

    When scenes will change, and ties are broken.

        Broken ?

        No, no,

        Not so,

      There still will be some tie.

2

Kind hearts are not too far away,

    Some token of good-will to send us,

Though some will go, and some must stay,

    Still as of old may God defend us ;

        Good-bye ?

        No, no,

        Not so,

    Good-night—ah ! not good-bye !

A MAGIC FIELD

1

A field, a field, down in the west,

Green, open to the sun and air :

A gust of love, a throbbing breast,

I could not cross it but in prayer.

2

For ever on that plot of ground

Some angel touched away my tears,

And heavenly echoes rang around

The narrow arches of mine ears.

3

They sang me songs of anguish old,

Mute loves, and measures of delight :

I trod the fabled fleece of gold

In mail of more than human might.

4

For hate grew distant as a dream,

And sorrow shed a subtle bliss ;

Deep in my breast there swam a beam

Of faith and melting tenderness.

5

The dead, the living, e'en as one,

Seemed singing through the twilight-air :

Time withered with the rolling sun,

And solace crowned the brows of care.

6

I paused and stretched mine arms abroad,

And then wrote swiftly with my pen :

" He who has felt the peace of God

Can work without the praise of men."

SEHNSUCHT

1

Fresh, fresh as a rose is the face of the Earth,

Immortal, abiding, Protean,

The death of a shower is the dew of the birth

Of a song-bird's impefious pæan.

2

But unknown, unexplored is the core of the Earth,

Too abysmal for human discerning :

Though her surface be flattered with seasons of
mirth,

Her breast is remorselessly burning.

3

But fairest of all is the rose of the Earth,

Man—man—Nature's prodigal giant :

The death of a dream is to him but the birth

Of resolve, philosophic, defiant.

4

But unplumbed is man's mystery still, though the
worth

Of his years be consumed in the learning ;

Like the central sad fires of his mother, the Earth :

His bosom is wasted with yearning.

A PAGAN CHORALE

Vex not thy soul with dread of death's accruing,
　Hush! hush all sorrows in forgetfulness ;
Weep not in dreams, the past is past pursuing,
　The future but a vain elusive guess ;
Let poppy twine thy tares, when the last embers
　Of life's gray fires drop on the cold hearth-stone :
Sleep! and dismiss the spirit that remembers
　All that thy days have done or left undone.

Come heavenly sleep, sink gently on his eyelids,
　O Hermes! touch his forehead with thy wand,
And guide him kindly when the last low sigh bids
　Thy presence waft him to a world beyond.

A BOY'S DAY-DREAM

All day he sat beside the pond,

And none rebuked ; for none could guess

The boy's retreat : no careless feet

Broke in upon his solitude ;

The cuckoo and the wilderness

Were the grand masons of his mood ;

With bricks of water, and airy mortar,

He built a turret and gazed beyond.

A thousand spirits he had, that gleam

Or creep or swim or live by the chase :

And magic spells from mystic wells

That hold in leash the skipping fays ;

Such made obeisance to his grace,

And fast as ants in Autumn days,

With song and sod, with trowel and hod,

They reared the battlement of dream.

3

A parapet of delicate make

With loop-holes cleft at intervals

Crowned the great tower ; and here a bower

A misty staircase led unto :

And from the summit a fountain falls

Of rainbow bubbles and drizzling dew :

And over the fountain, vista of mountain,

Blue sky, and beauty—his thirst to slake.

4

The boy gazed up, his large gray eyes

Absorbed in speculation : Lo—

Sudden there stood upon the flood

A naked figure, athletic, slim,

Flushed with the glory of love aglow

For a whiter phantom, that shadowed dim,

Beyond the fountain, beyond the mountain ;

Half seen, half veiled behind the skies.

5

The fountain figure stretched his arms,

Crying aloud : " My heart will break !—

If thou art real, O white ideal,

Stoop down and kiss me lest I die ;

Stoop and caress."—He seemed to wake

A million echoes with his cry :

And fairy fountain, figure and mountain

And tower collapsed in loud alarms.

TO A YOUNG POET

1

A voice! a voice! do you not hear it ringing

O'er fen and fold?

A poet's voice, do you not hear him singing

The new, and old?

2

I saw him lying, laughing in the clover,

Though none was near;

The meadows cry'd: "Welcome! the world's true
lover

Is here, is here."

3

All down the green glade late and early roaming,

In leafy grove,

I heard him softly singing: in the gloaming

He sang of love.

SIR HUMPHREY GILBERT'S LAST VOYAGE

" Sail on my bark, my bark sail on,

The moon is fled, the stars are gone."

        The lightnings quiver,

        The tempest shrieks :

        The yard-arms shiver,

        The cordage creaks.

" Furl sail, batter down the hatches:"

" Master, the hurricane catches us,

Master, the hurricane snatches us ! "

" Sail on my bark, my bark sail on,

Until the storm be overblown :

Little I reck of wrack or rent,

The five bells chime, the night is spent."

        " A shout, a shout,

        Put about, put about,

        A sailor overboard."

" Nay, leave him to the Lord,

For ship and soul on sea or land

Are close to God's almighty hand :

Sail on my bark, my bark sail on,

The moon is dead, the stars have flown ;

When the great storm of storms is past,

Man's destiny will clear at last."

His strength is weak,

His currents crossed ;

" A leak, a leak,

We're lost, we're lost ! "

" Master, the stern crushes in on us,

Master, the sea rushes in on us,

Lost, lost, all lost ! "

" Lost,—nay not lost, the haven's won,

Sink, sink, my bark, thy course is done,

For ship and soul on sea or land

Are close to God's almighty hand."

L

NATURE'S ETHICS

1

And when my brain is overwrought
With toil or solitary thought,
When all my fevered pulses beat,
And this flesh-prison throbs and thrills,
I sit beside the window-seat
Where oft I sat in boyhood's days,
And through the frost-bound silence, gaze
Upon the white majestic hills.

2

So meek, so stern, so wondrous still
They stand: they fortify my will
With strength the world knows nothing of;
With haughty silence to endure,

And with sincerity, to prove

That Nature's work knows no regrets,

She never falters or forgets,

Her paths are plain, her purpose sure.

3

Behind man's riot and life's folly,

Life's failure and man's melancholy,

Broods the great destiny, the plan

Slowly unfolded hour by hour

In Nature, and the soul of man ;

This is not changed, nor disappears,

But rules the rolling of the spheres,

And whispers through the frailest flower.

THE POPLARS

1

Not a voice, not a sound of the step of men,

    The shadowy kine on the uplands lie:

Not a bird is heard, not a stir from the glen,

    But only the slender poplars sigh.

2

On the hard white road glints the cusp of the moon,

    The land is cool'd with the wind's caress:

There is joy on all of the choral June,

    And the poplars utter their happiness.

3

For summer speaks to the world once more,

    Her music moves on the wings of the breeze,

O Love! thou art queen, from the sap and the core

    To the tips of the musical poplar-trees.

4

O mystical love! O magic unsung,

   That thy sorceress-spirit in secrecy weaves!

Ah! where among men is the silver-sweet tongue

   To sing us the song of the poplar-leaves?

(THE SONG)

(1)

Then fly with me; my love, with me;

   June, June is ours, I love, I yearn :

A land of flowers, and reverie,

   The poplars lisp love's low nocturn.

(2)

Ah! it must ever come to this,

   When love and youth and summer meet:

To wake a smile, to win a kiss,

   I'd cast an empire at thy feet.

(3)

Where thou art, the immortals are,

To breathe thy sweet Elysian breath

Would make a glow-worm grow a star,

And teach a dastard scorn of death.

(4)

Thy tones are like that solemn lyre

The stress of Nature speaketh through,

Thine eyes are moons of mellow fire,

Thy mouth a moss-rose moist with dew.

(5)

O come with me ; my love, with me :

June, June will die, I sigh, I yearn ;

Ope to the night's fond witchery,

My lily of the golden urn.

(6)

Steep me with nectar of thy mind,

Love's aromatic chalice spill :

No third is here : only a wind

Keeps tryst upon the moon-lit hill.

(7)

O earth, O earth, how strange thou art,

How new-created all that is ;

When love, fore-gathering at the heart,

First trembles in a mutual kiss.

DOWN STREAM

I

Who would not drift on such a stream
  At such an hour, alone with thee,
Together, you and I, Marie,
  Who would not drift, who would not dream ?
A while ago the full sun sank.
  And twilight gathered in the trees,
The slender reeds on either bank,
  With summer piped: " Say, who are these
That, dropping down an odorous wind,
  Slide smoothly past my rushy coves ? "
" We leave a world of tears behind
  In search of secret treasure-troves : "
The swimming lilies softly sighed :
  " 'Tis but a lover and his bride."

2

"We are alone. Still, as of old,

  To hear thy voice above the flood,

Ten times ten thousand strings of gold,

  Dear Marie, throb and thrill my blood.

But thou art as a faultless flower

  That sheds still perfume on the air,

What time the bee from manna-bower

  Wings forth, and searches everywhere :

And still the slim white throated flower

  Utters no sound, divinely dumb,

She rests on Nature's secret power.

  She knows the bee is sure to come :

So thou, sweet mistress, hast the art

  Of silence to enchant the heart.

3

"I've watched the goldfinch in the mead

  With fluttered palpitating wings

Poised close above the thistle-seed :

   And still he hovers, still she swings,

And still the winds, in captious play,

   Her crest incline, his feathers puff,

Where'er he turns, she bends away;

   And every slip and shy rebuff

But makes his hunger keener felt;

   So, when I bow, and fain would press

My lips to hers, and fondly melt

   In speech no language can express,

She moves, and I, poor fool, must miss

   The music of my lady's kiss.

4

   " How did my love begin?—a gleam

     From paradise that shot, and spread

Within my soul: a heavenly beam

     Pulsing in waves of joy and dread:

Ah! bid this deep majestic stream

Flow back, and seek his fountain-head.

We met : for better or for worse :

For worse ? Ah ! no, it cannot be,

Love needs must take its own sweet course

   In light and shadow to the sea ;

But ask not love's immortal source.

5

"Adown the maiden mountain-beck

   I've watched the eddies wreathe and swirl,

And scented bells of heather speck

   The dimpled flood : so coil and curl

The ringlets round thy slender neck,

   While drifts of fancy flush and fleck

The claustral cheek, the gates of pearl.

6

" Look up, Marie, this is our tryst :

   Away, away o'er stream and glen,

Ringed round and cloaked in cloud and mist,

Moves the great world of other men :

O let me be thy world alone,

As thou art mine, and only mine,

My heart shall be thy single throne,

Sole home, thy soul, so I am thine."

7

"O hold me and fold me belovèd,

I love thee :

If still thou must doubt me, then try me,

Then prove me :

O love, the subduer, will change not

With fashion,

Say, which is the truer, the world or

My passion :

As twilight with moonlight when daylight

Is over,

So eyesight wakes soul-sight in maiden

And lover ;

Let fortune caress thee; sin, sorrow

    Oppress me :

Still, still must I follow and worship

    And bless thee :

O silent, still doubting! then test me

    And prove me :

But, hold me and fold me, belovèd,

    I love thee."

8

" Aye, and thou love me, as thou art,

    So fresh and pure, so proud and fair,

And if thou give me all thine heart

    This moment as thou liest there,

Thou of thy single self shalt prove,

    Men grow immortal when they love.

9

" The earth will crumble like the past,

    Dead are the dreams of long ago,

How little may the present last !

  'Tis come and gone ere one can know :

A glance, a gleam, a moment's quiver

  Of moonlight on a flowing river.

10

"And shall this gaudy world mislead

  The man who sighs for sober rest ?

Ambition, Fortune, fame ?—indeed

  I find them all upon thy breast,

And in sincere simplicity

  Utterly give myself to thee.

11

"Death's finger cannot touch the bough

  That hangs in love's celestial bower ;

Love's life is an immortal now,

  A present never-dying hour.

When love and time meet ; in their kiss,

  Eternity is all that is."

OCTOBER—GOOD-BYE

1

The small brown brook swirls rapidly,

And gathered are the barley-sheaves :

Amid a fall of fading leaves

Our footsteps meet to say good-bye !

2

Come, let us stand where the road runs nigh

This side the heavy whitewashed gate,

Where wet square ricks stand desolate,

There let us wish and kiss good-bye !

3

The loose-leaf'd willows lean and sigh

Along the field where the brown brook flows,

How soon the day draws to its close !

How soon 'tis time to say good-bye !

4

Let us be resolute, and try
To find some utterance for relief;
Nor wrapt in mist of mournful grief,
Wait, dumb like cattle—you and I !

5

Loitering alone here, you and I
Can find no fond exchange of words:
We hang as silent as the birds,
It is so sad to say good-bye !

6

Needs must, from this low-weeping sky
I chase your twittering swallow south;
One last sweet silence, mouth to mouth:
Friends once, friends ever ! Love, good-bye !

AUTUMN TOUCHES

1

Now drops the fir-cone from the fir,

Ripe acorns patter through the oaks,

And half dismantled stands the wood,

The blue jay screams, the bull-frog croaks :

Safe garnered is the golden corn,

And glossy starlings boldly dash

And strip the scarlet mountain-ash,

The red may-berry hangs forlorn.

2

Where late stream'd tongues of scented bloom

Black hang the laburnum's shrivell'd pods,

The elm-tree sheds her small firm leaves,

The slim mast-poplar, naked, nods :

M

The orchard stands despoiled of fruit,

And barren boughs begin to show

Thick clumps of sage-green mistletoe,

While all the meads are moist and mute.

3

The filbert slips its russet sheath,

And walnut boughs are beaten bare,

A white mist crawls from vale to vale,

And shrewdly bites the evening air,

Tired flocks at twilight steal to fold ;

With burrowing mole the soil is loose,

And now the plough-boy sets his noose,

And earth-worms cast the mounded mould.

4

Dimpled with bent and willow-leaf,

O'er bedded reeds the shallow stream,

'Twixt tiny isle and shelving bank

Where dace in summer bask and gleam,

Runs and will run, till Boreas blow

His boisterous clarion through the gloom,

And cloak his course and seal his doom

With thickening frost and furious snow.

5

Cold hangs the nest beneath the thatch

Where late the circling swallow hung,

Weak linnets cloud the homestead ricks,

The sparrow pecks the farmyard dung;

Now hums the farmer's threshing-wheel,

And village children with their books

Peep in to watch the tossing stooks,

Then scamper away to mid-day meal.

6

The cub-fox knows his secret lair,

The hedgehog rolls himself to rest,

The cold snake curls beneath the leaves,

The mouse has weaved her winter nest,

Amid the thicket chirps the wren

And brusquely flits from twig to twig,

Dumb is the shrill high-elbowed grig,

The hare creeps down the marshy fen.

7

Thus all things, after their own kind,

Serve and preserve, bloom and decay :

Shall man alone, gifted with mind.

Swerve from his own appointed way ?

Because of knowledge shall he fail,

Or mazed in larger ignorance,

Neglect the will, bow down to chance,

And let the cruder form prevail ?

8

For each has some peculiar gift,

His bounden duty to perform :

O Earth ! and can a man not lift

That which is loosened by a worm !

Shall Nature stretch an arm to save

Her meaner creatures, teach them how

To toil and thrive : yet let man go,

Mocked with half-knowledge, to the grave ?

No! wider knowledge needs must print

A fuller faith upon the heart :

As hidden ways of Nature hint

Deep touches of diviner art:

'Tis good to grasp the facts of time

And search the secrets of the dust,

If but to trace how greed and lust

Expand by law, and learn to climb.

10

But shall mankind drop back and serve

The beggarly elements whence he rose,

Deny the soul, because he knows

This frame, too well, of flesh and nerve :

Shall he malign his long ascent,

And let despair or passion sway:

Nor bid the loftier spirit play

On this self-conscious instrument ?

11

No, no! For though man's ancient pride

Stand stript, and autumn skies be dull;

I will not sigh as once I sighed,

As once I wept, I will not weep:

Dead forms and faces beautiful

Still gather at the wells of sleep:

Wistful, but not disconsolate

I watch the leaves drop. Rest! tired earth!

In thy decay a better birth

Quickens, and I will love and wait.

MEDIOCRITY ANSWERED

He drifts and dies who has no aim,
Tost to and fro on buffeting seas:
Better to chase the pinioned flame
Of selfish purpose, better shame
With strength—than sink in sapless ease.

2

But better far, who with shut ears
Faces his moody thoughts alone;
Few hopes survive, but fewer fears
Confuse him as the end appears,
He looks ahead without a groan.

3

We have one life, but one to spend.

How shall we use the precious loan?

Dawn is our slave, the noon a friend,

Sunset may stay: but at the end

The soul must judge the soul alone.

4

Wilt keep the same our fathers had,

Treasure the buried talent?—but

Read the old page of Nature, shut

The book without a note to add,

And plod tradition's crudded rut?

5

"Ah! but I have no worthy gift,

No genius, learning, eloquence,

I am not strong, I am not swift,

I have not power enough to lift

This weight of conscious impotence.

6

" If I had only half your might,

Your courage, your unswerving will,

I'd dare defiance, in the fight

My sword should aid the cause of right:—

But now my life is like a mill

7

" That slowly moves its measured round,

Monotonously confident;

The stream, alas, is not profound,

The average weight of grain is ground;

Such was the wheel's predestined bent."

8

" Can then life's mill no freedom have ?—

What stream so hidd'n but stars will steal

And glimmer somewhere on the wave :

E'en if the wheel be but a slave,

Whence comes the stream that feeds the wheel ?

9

"What seems so now confined and slow

Far up the mountain-height outbroke

With godlike energy, aye, we know

Which way the element will flow,

When it has passed beyond the yoke.

10

"Why weigh the worth of small and great?

Water's the same the whole world through,

The deepest seas plunge desolate,

And heaven itself, in spite of fate,

Can gather in one drop of dew."

LINE BROTHERS, PRINTERS, CLACTON-ON-SEA.